COMPROMISED BRIDE MONTANA

Compromised Brides series

Cheryl Wright

Copyright

Montana
(Compromised Brides series)

Copyright ©2022 by Cheryl Wright

Small Town Romance Publications

Cover Artist: Silver Sage Book Covers

Dedication

To Margaret Tanner, my very dear friend and fellow author, for her enduring encouragement and friendship.

To Alan, my husband of over forty-eight years, who has been a relentless supporter of my writing and dreams for many years.

To You, my wonderful readers, who encourage me to continue writing these stories. It is such a joy knowing so many of you enjoy reading my stories as much as I love writing them for you.

Table of Contents

Chapter One

Egerton, Montana – 1880's

It took all her strength for Montana Brown to push her assailant away.

Rufus Hawk was a big man, and he was strong – far stronger than her.

He'd backed Montana into a corner in the barn, and try as he might, hadn't quite managed to get her onto the bale of hay. "I said no, Rufus!" she screeched, but it made no difference. Rufus had a reputation, and Montana should have heeded the warnings. Never be alone with him, was what she'd been told. Well, she wasn't alone. She was visiting with her horse, Trixie. In truth, the horse belonged to her fiancée, but he'd gifted her the horse when they'd got engaged.

"What is going on here?" Lester Brooks bellowed and suddenly Rufus jumped back, releasing Montana from his grip.

The shock on his face was momentary. Then he wore a smirk. "Montana couldn't keep her hands off me," he said, turning toward the man she was to marry.

"That's a lie!" With trembling hands, Montana fumbled with the buttons on her blouse – some were still in place, others torn away. "Do you think I would tear my own clothing?" Tears filled her eyes as she noted the rage on Lester's face. His fist connected with Rufus' jaw before she could blink an eye. Lester hurried to Montana and helped her up, his arms going around her then walked her into the house. They left Rufus laying flat out on the ground, he then walked her into the house.

Despite the sounds of the townsfolk surrounding them, Lester ignored it all. If his parents hadn't offered to hold the church picnic on their property, none of this would have happened.

He sat her near the fire, then wrapped a blanket around Montana's shoulders. "I'll get you a mug of tea," he said. He returned shortly afterwards, his mother following behind.

"Montana," Gertrude Brooks snapped. "You've really done it this time." *Done what?* She was a victim of that revolting Rufus Hawk. Montana couldn't even bring herself to call him a man. "I cannot allow you to marry my son after what you and Rufus did." She pursed her lips and glared at Montana as though she were a snake in the grass.

"Nothing happened. Lester…"

Lester interrupted. "Mother! This is not Montana's fault." He leaned down and put his arms around her, in a show of support for his future wife.

Gertrude Brooks turned on her heels and left the room, returning moments later with her husband, a smug look on her face. "You have a choice, Son," Harold Brooks said firmly. "This… this… harlot, " he said grimly. "Or your inheritance." Lester's parents then left the room, ceasing all discussion.

Her fiancée turned to Montana, a look of shock on his face. "I'm sorry, Montana," he said. "Looks like the wedding is off."

Montana couldn't believe Lester had dumped her after Rufus had put her in a compromising position. Choosing his inheritance over her was appalling, and they both knew it. Thinking about it, she should have known. His parents had hated her from the start.

If she'd been from the right side of town, things would have been different. Her family was not rich like Lester's and that was the problem. His mother had been looking for an excuse to get rid of her from the moment the pair began stepping out. When this unfortunate situation arose, she should have known it was the end. Lester loved money. As it turned out, he loved it far more than he loved Montana.

What she would do now, she did not know.

She could, of course, stay in town with her tail between her legs, but that wasn't in Montana's nature. Not convinced she could take the embarrassment of the gossip that was sure to spread, she opted to leave instead.

Not being in the wrong, she shouldn't even contemplate leaving, but if she knew Gertrude Brooks, Lester's mother, word would quickly spread that she seduced her attacker. The fact she'd been a victim of a man who had raped several women didn't seem to bother Mrs. Brooks. It was funny – everyone thought her an upstanding citizen, but in reality, the woman was a viper, and not one to be reckoned with.

She stood on the train platform with her meagre luggage. The memory of her mother's anguish was still heavy in her heart. None of it was her fault, but Montana knew she would be punished for the rest of her days should she stay in Egerton.

Her head shot up as she heard the train whistle in the distance. This was it – wherever she landed, no one would know her history. The fact she was a compromised woman would not enter their heads. She could start anew with her head held high.

Sadness overcame Montana as she realized she could never marry, and therefore, never have children. She fought back tears as she stepped onto the near empty train. Her ticket would take Montana to the end of the line, but where she alighted was another thing altogether.

Would she ever find somewhere to call home, or would Egerton forever be on her mind?

"Miss, Miss!" Montana wasn't sure if it was the loud voice that woke her, or the shaking. "Everyone needs to get off the train, Miss," the man said.

Her eyes opened in astonishment as she glanced around. When had she fallen asleep? Montana had a little money on her, but not too much, and had decided to keep her wits about her. Otherwise, she could be robbed in her sleep.

She grabbed up her reticule, relieved to discover it hadn't been tampered with, but where were they? She couldn't see a station platform. "What's going on?" she asked, her voice still husky from sleep.

The stranger stopped shaking her and stared. "We're stuck in the middle of nowhere. That's where. Train robbers set a fire on the tracks and everyone needs to get off."

Montana cringed. "Train robbers? Are we safe?" She clutched tightly to her reticule as though it were the fountain of life. Of course, to her, it was. It held enough money to see her through for a couple of weeks, at least. For some, that was a fortune. For her, it was the price Lester paid to rid himself of her. To force her to leave town without causing trouble.

Not only was she compromised, but she was paid off as though she were a common whore. How did she ever get mixed up with that shadow of a man? Montana was certain she would never know.

Finally fully awake, Montana looked the stranger over. She'd thought he was the conductor. This man did not wear any sort of uniform. She glanced about. The rest of the carriage was empty. *Where was everyone? Why were they the only two people still there?*

Her heart pounded. Something was very wrong, but in her half asleep stupor, Montana couldn't quite fathom what that was.

The stranger grabbed her arm and tried to drag her off her seat. Montana resisted, but he lifted her into his arms. "We have to get out of here, Miss. The robbers are coming." His grin told her otherwise. She stared up into his face. He was unshaven and had the most disgusting odor. This man was no conductor, and she struggled.

"Let me go! Put me down!" she screeched, but he continued to grin.

"You're mine now," he said, moving his lips close to hers. Montana balked at the foul smell coming from his mouth.

"Over my dead body," she screamed, but he only laughed.

Never in her wildest dreams did Montana believe anything like this could happen. It was clear she couldn't escape, but she certainly wasn't going to go down without a fight. That wasn't in her nature.

The man carried her through the carriage, then passed her down to someone else. "You got you a feisty one there, Boss," the other man said, then handed her back when the *boss* was on even ground.

She had no idea why, but Montana continued to clutch her reticule. They were certain to take her money, but terror built up inside her when she realized it wasn't all they would take.

Her heart pounded so loud it felt like it would jump right out of her chest, to the point she'd become light-headed. The distant sound of horse's hooves terrified her. *Were more robbers arriving, or was she about to be saved from the clutches of hell?* Montana silently prayed it was the latter. She'd been through so much lately. She was saved from Rufus, only to find herself in a far more precarious situation.

What had she done to deserve this? Montana closed her eyes against whatever fate awaited her. She was helpless against this man, against whatever he had planned for her. Deep down, Montana knew exactly what he wanted from her She also knew she would never recover. Tears flooded her eyes, but she wouldn't let them fall. Instead, she pummeled his chest, his arms, his face, until he stopped in his tracks.

"Damn you, woman! Stop it," he yelled. When she didn't, he put her to the ground and slapped her hard. So hard Montana saw stars. It wasn't what she'd had in mind. The plan in her head was to deter him, convince him to let her go. Only this man was clearly a hardened criminal. That was easy to see. Amateurs did not rob trains. They did not corral the passengers into a corner and hold guns on them. And they certainly didn't choose one woman to make their own and take their pleasure with them. Even if that was only on a short-term basis.

It was then Montana realized she wasn't getting out of this alive. This man would do whatever he wanted with her, then kill her. No one would ever be the wiser.

Bile rose in her throat, and Montana brought up her breakfast. The fact it was all over her kidnapper pleased her immensely.

"You witch!" he screamed.

His fellow robbers stood gawking. Montana was lightheaded with fear, and despite her best efforts, her chin trembled. "It's your fault," she said with an unsteady voice. "You didn't have to hit me." Tears streamed down her face now, and she didn't care.

Right now, her life was in danger. She watched as he dragged his pistol from its holster.

"Hold it right there, Tritton." Montana was frozen with fear and hadn't heard anyone else arrive. "Miss," the man said firmly, addressing Montana. "Make your way over here." She was terrified and couldn't think straight. "Miss," he said again, more loudly and far more urgently this time.

Montana glanced up to see at least a dozen men on horseback, all yielding a rifle. They far outnumbered the robbers. She was shaking uncontrollably and unable to move, so instead he brought his horse forward, then reached down and swung her up behind him on the horse.

Montana watched as the robbers threw down their guns, including the one who'd held her hostage. "Are you alright, Miss?" her rescuer asked. He glanced back at her momentarily when she didn't answer. "Miss?"

She swallowed hard. "I… I think so," she said in a quiet voice. "Thank you for saving me."

He touched his hat, but didn't say another word. The men who rode with him climbed down from their horses and handcuffed the gang.

She watched as the male passengers cleared the fire from the tracks, and the train was soon moving again. Marshal Colt Harris, her rescuer, rode the train with Montana. His horse was taken back to town by the posse.

Chapter Two

"I… I didn't see anything," Montana said. "I was asleep." She licked her lips, and he watched her every move.

"You were vulnerable, easy prey." Colt had taken her back to his office when they'd arrived in town. The train was far more comfortable for her than the back of his horse, he was certain. His deputy placed a mug of coffee in front of the woman, then handed one to him.

"I'm Marshal Colt Harris," he said. "And you are?"

She stared at him then, as though he was asking for all her worldly goods. "Montana Brown."

"Montana like the state?"

She sighed. He guessed it was a common question. "Yeah. My parents thought it was funny. It isn't."

He nodded and gave a little grunt. People could be stupid, but this took the cake. "Well, Miss Brown, I've arranged for you to stay at the local women's boarding house. We have retrieved your luggage from the train station." He indicated her luggage sitting in the corner of the room. "But I need to be certain you are unharmed." He studied her then. She was deathly pale, which was understandable, given the circumstances. Apart from that, she appeared unharmed.

She sighed again. Colt decided she was exhausted after her ordeal. "His foul breath harmed me immensely," she said, then a small smile played on her lips. At least she could joke about it. "I know I was lucky. I can't thank you enough for rescuing me."

It was then he noticed the tears dancing on her eyelids. It was his turn to sigh. Colt couldn't abide crying women. It was an aversion he had, mostly because he didn't know how to handle them. *Did he hand them a handkerchief and let them sob their hearts out, or did he take them in his arms and let them cry against his chest?*

Women were delicate flowers. His mother told him that when he was a teenager. She also told him he had to treat women with care. He'd been out with women here and there, but none appealed to him, so he really didn't know what to do or how to behave when it came to women.

He opted to hand her his handkerchief. Instead of taking it, she glared at him, then swiped at her face. This was a feisty one. He could see that.

The best thing he could do was to keep his distance. He stood. "Let's go to the boarding house," he said, and grabbed her luggage before she could protest.

Miss Mae Wilson was a little older than one might expect to see in a person running a boarding house, but to Colt, she was perfect. She was just the right balance of firm, friendly, and motherly. She ensured the women living there were well fed and looked after, but kept them in check. There were curfews she expected them to abide by, but was always available for a bit of motherly advice.

Colt knocked on the front door and waited for Miss Mae to let them in. He didn't have to wait long. "Miss Mae, hello again."

The elderly woman studied Montana from head to toe. "My dear girl," she said, taking Montana by the hand. "Do come inside. You've had a terrible ordeal, I can tell." Montana appeared startled, but Miss Mae put her at ease. "Come into the kitchen. I have a lovely cup of tea waiting for you, and coffee for the Marshal."

"I don't have time…"

"Of course you do, Marshal. You can take a moment or two to sit and have a slice of cake, surely?" She threw him a sly smile then. The one that Colt knew meant he needed to stay.

"Where should I put Miss Brown's luggage?" There was little of it, but it would be good to put it down.

"Top of the stairs, second door to the right. Thank you, Marshal."

Colt hurried up the stairs and left Montana's luggage inside the door. The room was homely and looked comfortable. He hoped Montana would feel relaxed there. Although, after what she'd been through, he was doubtful that would happen. He hurried back downstairs. The thought of Miss Mae's cake had him drooling. She was an excellent cook, and he rarely passed up an offer to eat there, but today he had paperwork to do. It was sheer luck no one had been injured during that robbery today. Miss Montana Brown was particularly lucky. If black smoke hadn't been spotted out of town, he wouldn't be any the wiser about what was transpiring.

He shook his head. Jack Tritton was a hardened criminal who took whatever he wanted. That could be money, jewelry, and even women. The law, and that included Colt, had been trying to catch up with the Tritton gang for nearly a year. They were smart – at least as smart as criminals go – moving from town to town, but along the same train line. They were bound to be caught. The man had terrorized far too many travelers, but most of all women. The man simply took what appealed to him.

The gang, at least those involved in the train robbery, were locked up in the jailhouse, and the stench was overwhelming. If he had the choice, Colt would throw soapy water over the lot of them. The jailhouse had never reeked so badly.

"Sit down, Marshal," Miss Mae told him. "I have carrot cake, freshly baked this morning." She handed him a slice on a sparkling white plate, then placed a mug of coffee in front of him.

Montana Brown sat opposite him and looked like she was ready to fall in a heap. His mother was right when she'd said women were delicate flowers. To be fair, she had been through a traumatic experience. If the posse hadn't turned up when they did, goodness knew what might have happened to her.

He shuddered at the thought.

Colt studied the young woman, who looked as though she would jump at her own shadow. "How are you feeling, Miss Brown?" He kept his voice quiet to ensure he didn't startle her.

Miss Mae glared at him. "How do you think she's feeling? That brute of a man accosted her, and we all know what his intentions were. At least here she is safe and sound."

Colt could have slapped himself. Miss Mae was right, of course. To his detriment, he hadn't thought before he spoke. "I apologize, Miss." he said, barely able to look the young woman in the eye. She seemed to wilt under his gaze.

She straightened herself and studied him. "There's nothing to apologize for," she replied, but Colt knew that was untrue.

He lifted his coffee mug, studying her over the top. Colt felt certain if he wasn't there, she'd turn into a blubbering mess. But who was he to judge? He didn't know Miss Montana Brown. He didn't know how she usually looked, and he certainly did not know her life experiences.

One thing he was certain of, she'd not been kidnapped by a criminal before. He would monitor her and ensure she really was fine. He scratched his head. Too late now, but he should have insisted the Doc check her over. "I should get the Doc," he suddenly blurted out.

Both women suddenly stared at him. "Yes, you should," Miss Mae said firmly.

"I'm perfectly fine," Miss Brown said. "I'm not harmed, I promise." Her eyes pleaded with him, and he turned to Miss Mae for support.

"It's up to Miss Brown," she said, not quite so firmly this time. He should have known she'd take the side of another woman.

Colt drained his coffee mug and finished his piece of cake. "Thank you, Miss Mae. That was delicious. I need to get back to the piles of paperwork a train robbery produces."

"Not to mention an attempted kidnapping," Miss Brown whispered.

"Judge Ravin should be here in a day or two. You'll be required to testify, then you're free to leave town."

Montana Brown's mouth dropped open. "I…" She seemed far more shocked now than at the time of the robbery. She suddenly closed her mouth again, then took a sip of tea.

It was obvious she hadn't thought about this possibility. He needed her to put Tritton away for the rest of his life. The other women, those he did kidnap and taken back to his lair, were far too traumatized to testify. They had even found some of the kidnapped women brutally murdered.

Colt was relying on Miss Brown to have the beast locked up for the rest of his life. Or better still, hanged.

"We need you Miss Brown. Your participation in the trial should be over with in a matter of minutes. Then you are free to leave."

Colt stood then, and without another word, left the boarding house.

Montana snuggled down into the luxurious bed. There was only herself and Miss Mae at the boarding house, which should make her plan simple.

If there'd been a lot of women staying there, her plan may have been thwarted. This way, it would be easy to pull off.

Despite the cold early morning chill, she slid out of her warm bed. Breakfast would be nice, but Montana needed to get away before anyone was alerted to her disappearance. Her timing needed to be precise. If she left too early, it would be obvious she was leaving. Waiting at the stage depot could give her away. If that happened, Marshal Harris would likely haul her back to the boarding house.

She swallowed back her fear. Montana was terrified. Not of testifying, but of what may happen if they released any of the gang. Right now, the entire gang were locked up in the jailhouse. If the judge let any of them out, they could, and likely would, retaliate against her. And where would she be then?

No, she couldn't hang around here. Harrigan's Pass was a small place. By now, everyone who lived there would know of her existence. Her heart pounded. Montana couldn't risk staying. It could be the end for her.

She dressed and packed up her few belongings, then slipped downstairs. The aroma of freshly baked biscuits wafted through the house, but she had to resist. The stagecoach was due to leave in only a few minutes. If she didn't hurry, it would leave without her.

Montana opened the door slowly, being as quiet as she could. Closing it equally silently would be the problem. She put her luggage on the ground and pulled the door closed as gently as she could. She flinched at the click she heard, but had to assume Miss Mae didn't hear it over the rattle of dishes in the kitchen.

She hurried down the street and arrived at the stage depot just in time to buy a ticket and board before it left. Montana did not know where she was headed, but provided she was leaving Harrigan's Pass, which she was, she didn't care. She only wanted to get as far away from there as she could.

Two elderly women were already aboard the stagecoach and looked her up and down. "Good morning, my dear," one woman said.

"Where are you headed?" the other woman asked.

Montana didn't know, and had to think. "Anywhere but here," she finally answered, then realized that probably wasn't the best thing to tell a complete stranger.

"You poor girl," the older of the two women said. "A broken heart. I can relate to that. The further away you get, the better. You never know, you might find your soulmate on the other side of the county."

Montana nodded, but knew that wouldn't be true. She thought she'd found her soulmate, but he dumped her for a big fat inheritance. Then she'd been kidnapped with a view too… Tears filled her eyes. The past days had been a nightmare. She'd gone from one catastrophe to another, and neither one was her fault.

The stagecoach door slammed shut, and she jumped. "My dear girl," the slightly older woman said, then moved to sit beside Montana. She put her arms around her and comforted her. "They're not worth it," she said.

"My goodness," the other woman said. "We should introduce ourselves. I am Miss Millie Ranwell, and this is my sister Josephine Ranwell."

Montana wiped at her tears and glanced at them both. "I'm Montana Brown," she whispered. "My fiancée dumped me for his inheritance." It wasn't untrue, but it wasn't the reason she was leaving the tiny town of Harrigan's Pass. Montana was certain if the circumstances had been different, she would have likely stayed. It seemed like a lovely place, and except for Jack Tritton, the people she'd met had been nice to her.

Although it was not a lie, it wasn't true about this place, and she felt terrible. Everything that had happened recently seemed to suddenly come crashing down on her, and she began to sob. She was startled when the carriage moved.

"Ah, finally we're on our way," Miss Millie told her. She handed Montana a handkerchief. "Things will look better when we're away from town," she said. "That fiancée of yours is a fool. It is plain to see he did not appreciate you. A man like that doesn't deserve someone like you."

Was Miss Millie talking from experience? It appeared neither woman had ever married, although that was an assumption Montana had made. She studied the woman who held her like she cared. "Thank you," she said in a whisper. "I was in love with him. I thought he loved me too."

"Forget him," Miss Josephine said firmly. "He's not worth your time." Her lips were pursed, and she looked angry. Montana guessed she'd been through something similar. "From childhood, we are told we need a husband. It is not true," she said firmly. "Millie and I have lived as spinsters for many years. It hasn't done us any harm." She crossed her arms then and nodded. She didn't know what happened to these two caring women, but it was obvious they'd been crossed by a man.

"We'll be at Stratford soon," Miss Millie said. "We can grab a bite to eat before we continue to our next destination." That sounded good. Montana's belly was beginning to protest.

An hour later and they pulled into Stratford. The food there was delicious. After eating her fill, Montana used the privy, then returned to wait for the stagecoach. The sisters were waiting impatiently to board the stagecoach. "Oh, thank goodness," Miss Millie said. "The coach is about to leave. I thought you were going to miss it."

"Not likely. The further I get from Harrigan's Pass, the better," Montana said firmly.

"Of course," Miss Josephine said. "We're headed for Helena. Why don't you come with us? If you have no other plans, that is."

Montana thought for a moment. It wasn't a terrible idea. Helena was big enough for her to get lost in, and no one would find her. "That's sounds wonderful," she finally said. "I have a little money, so can pay my way until I can secure employment." It wouldn't do to let anyone know she had a wad of money in her reticule. Even these ladies who seemed above reproach. She'd trusted before, and look where that got her.

Right now, Helena seemed like the perfect answer.

Chapter Three

Marshal Colt Harris was tired.

And he was frustrated. Why on earth Miss Brown had fled town, he had no idea. She was safe where she was. The train robbers were locked up in his jail. From what he could tell, he had the entire gang, but he couldn't be certain.

That last thought made him pause. Was that why she ran? Did she think the rest of the gang would come after her?

He supposed it was possible, but Colt honestly believed he'd rounded them all up. It was highly unlikely Tritton would leave any of his men behind. Especially for a big job like a train robbery – he would need all available help for a job like that.

The sun was moving down the sky. Normally, he would have arrived at his destination by now. The buggy slowed him down. There was no chance he'd expect his horse to carry two people all the way back to Harrigan's Pass, especially after such a long trip to retrieve his witness.

He warred with himself about chasing after her, but in the end, decided the best course of action was to take her back to testify. Colt had better things to do.

Because she'd taken off, he still hadn't finished the paperwork. It would have been far easier if he'd wired ahead and had another marshal retrieve the woman, but not knowing what she looked like, they would work blind.

"It's alright, Nellie," he said soothingly. "We're almost there. We have no choice but to stay the night. By the time I catch up with Miss Montana Brown, it will be almost dark. Too dark to ride home again tonight." He was having a discussion with his horse. Of all the fool things to do, that had to take the cake.

Colt shook his head. The long trip was obviously getting to him.

If he'd calculated correctly, he should arrive in Stratford any minute. The stage was due to leave shortly. He would kick himself if he just missed it. The last thing he wanted to do tonight was chase down a stagecoach. Especially since the driver might believe it was a robbery. He shook his head again. Surely he wouldn't think that. How many robberies happened with the robber riding a buggy? He must be delusional even having such thoughts.

It wasn't long before he pulled into the stage depot. Colt breathed a sigh of relief to see the coach was still there. Waiting to climb aboard was a small group of women, but he couldn't see if Miss Brown was amongst them.

After securing the buggy and his horse, Colt hurried over to the awaiting passengers. He knew they had one more stop tonight before settling down for the night. Montana's head suddenly shot up. It was as though she sensed him there, and she hurried up the steps of the stagecoach, almost slipping as she rushed.

"My dear girl," he heard one of the older women say. "What on earth is wrong?"

Montana whispered something and retreated inside the carriage.

"You, Sir!" One woman turned on him. "Back off now!"

Colt glanced around. No one else was there, so it had to be him she was addressing. He pointed at his chest. "Are you addressing me, Madam?" he asked, feeling totally confused.

"Miss! She ground out. Miss Josephine Ranwell."

Colt could see he would have a fight on his hands. Montana had obviously rounded up assistance on the off-chance he found her.

"You, Sir, are a cad." Miss Ranwell lifted her skirts and turned away. She hurried up the steps and sat down next to Montana Brown. The other woman sat on the other side of the woman he was pursuing.

Confusion overtook him. What on earth had Miss Brown told them for him to be attacked like this? He hurried to the stagecoach and ensured the driver stayed put. The man wasn't happy, but when Colt produced his badge, complied.

Standing on the steps of the stagecoach, he studied Montana Brown, who sat inside. "Miss Brown, Montana," he said firmly. "I need you to come with me."

Miss Ranwell glared at him. "You dumped her once. What do you intend to do this time?" The woman's lips were pursed, and Colt felt sure she would shove him if they were face to face.

"Dump? I have no idea what you're…"

The other woman rounded on him then. "Oh, we know all about you. Leaving Miss Montana in the lurch." She also glared, then her eyes opened in astonishment. "You're a marshal! That's even worse."

"I don't…"

He stared at Montana. Her lips curled slightly, but he was still none the wiser.

"You need to marry her. Tonight. I'm certain the preacher would be amenable."

Colt felt himself pale. *Marry? Tonight?* What lies had Miss Brown been telling these women? When he glanced at her again, she was white as a ghost, and shaking her head.

"But I'm going with you to Helena," Montana told Miss Ranwell. "I'm don't want to marry *him*!" Then she slapped her hand to her mouth, as though she'd said too much.

Colt stared in disbelief as the two women argued over whether or not Montana should marry him. He couldn't believe this was happening. He'd come here to Stratford to retrieve a witness. How were things so twisted he found himself being married off? It was bizarre, not to mention downright scary.

"I have no intention of marrying anyone, let alone Miss Brown," he said forcefully. "You, Miss Ranwell, need to stand down." He then forced his way into the carriage and grabbed Montana by the arm, leading her out of the carriage.

She glanced at him, a barely visible smile on her lips. *What was she up to now?* The moment they stepped foot outside the carriage, he led her toward the buggy. Montana let out an almighty scream. She pierced him with her eyes. *What game was she playing?*

"Let me go and I'll stop," she whispered, then screamed again. The driver ran toward them, as did the two women she'd obviously been traveling with.

"Young man, you unhand that woman!" It was the other woman who spoke this time. Miss Millie Ranwell. "I know your kind – make all the promises in the world, have your way, then dump them."

He stared at her, opened mouthed. "Have my…" *What sort of foolishness was this?* "I just came to collect my…"

"If you are not prepared to marry your fiancée, she is coming with us." She lifted her chin and Colt could see how determined this old biddy was. All was becoming clear to him. She'd been left at the altar, and believed every man had an obligation to marry the woman he'd promised to marry. Only he had made no such promise. He scratched his forehead. Was there no way to get out of this situation? He needed to take Montana Brown back to Harrigan's Pass with him. There was no clue when the judge would arrive, but she needed to be there when he did.

"If I promise to marry her, will you let me take her?" He could see no other way to claim her and not have Montana scream the place down.

"I'm not marrying you," Montana said in a harsh whisper.

He stared down at her, partly amused, but mostly annoyed. "I'm not marrying you either. It's clear to me these ladies won't let me take you unless I promise to marry you," he whispered.

"That would be acceptable," the sisters said at precisely the same time.

Colt sighed with relief. "Good. You can leave now driver, but I'll need Miss Brown's luggage."

"And ours," the two women said.

"We can finish our trip tomorrow," Miss Josephine said with a satisfied smile on her lips.

"Lord, give me strength," Colt mumbled. *What were they up to now?*

The three women plus Colt stood inside the stage depot. "The preacher is still up," Miss Josephine said, a determined look on her face. "I can see the light from here."

Colt pulled Montana away from the two interfering older women. "You know I didn't promise to marry you. Why are you doing this?"

She stared up at him. Her brown eyes filled with fear. "I didn't say *you* were my fiancée. I only said my fiancée dumped me." She looked on the verge of tears, and that was the last thing he wanted. *Delicate flowers* kept forcing its way into his mind, and all he wanted to do was hold her close against him. Darn his mother for teaching him that!

He sighed again. "You know we're not getting out of this unscathed. Those two have us married off, and they're not going to let up. I can't see any choice but to go through with the marriage, then get an annulment. I know a judge who would do it." He winked at her then, and her shock was evident.

"I don't want to marry you," she ground out.

He didn't want to marry her, either. It was like a comedy scene playing out before their very eyes, only they were the characters, and they couldn't get out of it. "I don't want to marry you either. I'd rather find someone more amenable." The words were out of his mouth before he realized the ramifications of what he was saying.

Her entire demeanor changed at his words. Her eyes seemed to flare, and her lips pursed. "That's so wonderful," she suddenly said, then leaned in and held him. Suddenly she glanced up at him, her eyes full of mischief. She reached up and pulled him down to her, then kissed him full on the lips.

Colt resisted at first, but remembered the sisters were watching, and finally complied. It was all for show. Montana was against the marriage as much as he was. She was playing a part, and he needed to do his bit, too.

Her lips were soft, and she tasted sweet. He didn't know what she'd eaten, but it tasted good. She tasted good. He closed his eyes and everything else faded away. The two women screaming at him to marry Montana faded away, too. He pulled her a little closer, and she softly groaned.

Colt suddenly opened his eyes. What was he doing? He'd let himself get carried away by the moment. By the little witch standing in front of him. He might have saved her, but he sure as heck didn't want to be fooled by her, let alone marry her.

But that's exactly what he was going to have to do to get out of the situation he was in.

"Time to find that preacher," he announced. He looked up to see the two older women grinning.

Chapter Four

As they left the tiny church, Montana was dazed.

How it came to this, she wasn't certain. The sisters were definitely the instigators and wouldn't let up. Colt was not a compliant participant. From all accounts, he was not interested in getting married, whether that was to her or someone else entirely.

Mind you, he didn't balk when she kissed him. Well, for a moment or two, he did. Then he was right there, enjoying every moment. If she was truthful, Montana had enjoyed it, too.

No matter, they needed to get out of their predicament now. Once the meddling sisters were gone, Colt would arrange for an annulment. He seemed to think it would be simple, given his ties with the judicial. The same judge went to Harrigan's Pass every month, he said, and often more if necessary.

That certainly made her feel better. After her experience with Lester Brooks, the last thing Montana wanted was to be married… to anyone!

"How wonderful!" Miss Josephine exclaimed. "I do love a wedding." She was smiling almost from ear to ear.

"Except your own," Miss Millie said dryly. "We're thrilled for you both." She moved in and hugged Montana, but looked Colt up and down as though he were the bad guy. Montana almost laughed, except it was no laughing matter. The sisters were the very reason she was in this predicament. If they hadn't bullied Colt, they wouldn't be standing here now.

"Now to find a room," Miss Josephine said cheerfully. "Let's hope there's room at the hotel."

Miss Millie rolled her eyes. "Of course there will be room. Stratford is a one-horse town. The only visitors they would get would be from the stagecoach, and that's rare, I'm certain."

Colt herded them all toward the hotel. "Good evening," Colt said to the clerk. "We need some rooms."

"Two for my sister and I, and the honeymoon suite," Miss Josephine told the man.

He laughed. "We don't have a honeymoon suite, Miss," he said as he continued to chuckle.

"Then a double for the newlyweds," she retorted. Montana could feel the heat travel up her face.

"Singles will do," she protested.

"We're on our honeymoon, sweetheart," Colt said as he pulled her close against himself. "Separate rooms will never do," he finished, as he pulled her close. He winked then, and she wanted nothing more than to pound him. He was playing with her now, and Montana didn't like it one iota. "Once I get my wife settled in her room, I need to settle my horse. Can you give me directions?"

The clerk told Colt where he needed to go, and how to rouse the livery owner at this time of night. He explained about breakfast in the morning and told the sisters what time the next stagecoach would arrive.

The Ranwell sisters had been kind to Montana, but insisting the marshal marry her was unforgiveable. He was not happy, and neither was she. That wouldn't change until the annulment came through.

No matter what happened, she couldn't stay married to this man. She was a compromised woman, and there was no changing that. She had already resigned herself to the fact. At least with an annulment, she didn't have to worry. Besides, Colt Harris didn't love her, and she didn't love him, so what was the problem?

Colt settled her in their room, then reluctantly left to tend to Nellie.

Maybe they could go to the preacher in the morning and have their marriage registration removed. They could tear up the marriage certificate in front of him, and all would be well. By that time, the sisters would be gone, and would be none the wiser.

Montana sat on the edge of the double bed and sighed. That definitely sounded like a good plan. She would talk to Colt about it when he returned.

She glanced about the room. There was a sofa in the corner. Colt could sleep on that, only it was barely long enough for someone of her size, let alone a man as tall as her husband. *Her husband.* Montana wasn't sure she would ever get used to that.

The truth was, she didn't need to. First thing tomorrow, after waving the sisters goodbye, they would visit the preacher and the pair would no longer be married. What a relief that would be, not only for herself but also for the marshal, she was certain.

Right now, she wanted nothing more than to have a bath. To clean the dust from her skin and her hair, and to rid herself of the memory of that horrible man who had tried to kidnap her. She'd availed herself of the bath at Miss Mae's, but that vile man reeked. She couldn't shake the memory of his hands on her, and his foul breath near her lips.

Montana almost retched at the thought of it.

Despite Colt demanding she stay in their room with the door locked, Montana hurried down the hallway to the bathroom. She should have known there would be no running water in a dump like this. There was, however, a bowl and jug of water in their room, and that would have to do.

Montana filled the bowl and stripped down to her waist. The water was not warm, in fact it was bitterly cold, but would have to do. The hotel soap would be harsh on her skin, but it was better than having *that man's* touch on her. The thought made her tremble.

She rubbed the lye soap into the rough face cloth supplied, and rubbed it up and down her arms. She scrubbed at her skin until it was red. Montana couldn't bear the thought of Jack Tritton's hands on her, and she needed to wash every bit of her skin to eliminate his filth from her body. She was more than grateful to the marshal, to Colt, for saving her.

The fact she was grateful, did not mean she had to marry him. Tears sprung into her eyes. He was a good-looking man, quite handsome in fact. Had the circumstances been different, she may not have cared. But things being as they were, theirs could never be a proper marriage. It also meant she could never bear his children.

Merely thinking about it was heartbreaking. She had planned a family with Lester, but the cad shoved her aside for a pile of money. She was still shocked at what he'd done. Until that moment, she believed Lester truly loved her. Now it was apparent he loved money far more.

His parents had always hated her. They wanted someone *far better* to become his wife. Someone who was raised in high society, and could contribute to his family's fortune. That wasn't Montana.

The best thing she could do was forget about him and live her life the best way she could.

As she continued to scrub every inch of her skin, it struck her. *Had Lester's parents secured Rufus to attack her? To ruin her reputation and rid themselves of her?* They knew their son better than she did – and likely knew he'd take the money over her.

Oh, the shame of it all. With that revelation in mind, her situation seemed even worse than she originally thought.

Tears sprung to her eyes and there was nothing she could do to stop them. She continued to scrub her torso before the marshal returned. She was almost done when she heard the lock turn. She gasped. The door opened, and she spun to face him.

She froze. He stared at her.

Montana finally came to her senses and snatched up the stiff and worn towel and covered herself. Colt suddenly spun around and walked out the door again, slamming it behind him.

She would never get over the embarrassment.

"What are you doing out here?" Of all the people, it had to be Miss Josephine. Her voice really grated on him. "Well? Why aren't you in there with your bride?" Her hands on her ample hips, she pierced him with her eyes, and Colt nearly squirmed under her gaze. *What was it about the woman that had him almost on his knees to her every demand?*

This time, he stood his ground. "My wife is bathing." *Not that it's any of your business*, he wanted to add, but felt he would only make matters worse. "I'm giving her space."

Miss Josephine nodded. "I suppose at least you are being considerate. With Montana being a new bride and all." She harrumphed loudly, then returned to her room.

How did he get himself in this situation? That much was clear. Those busy-body women bullied him into it. Colt had dealt with hardened criminals, robbers, gangs, and even murderers. He treated them the way he was supposed to — with no mercy. Why then did he let these elderly women walk all over him?

He knew the answer before he even thought about it. Because he was raised properly. He was taught to treat women with respect. If he hadn't done that, his mother would have whipped his butt. And rightly so.

Because of that, he could not argue with those ladies, as frustrating and annoying as they were. Whatever Montana had told them, he knew it didn't apply to him. But who did it apply to? *Did that mean she was engaged to another man? What had he done to her? Dumped her by the sounds of things, but why?*

He knocked lightly on the door. "Miss Brown," he called, then realized the stupidity of calling his wife Miss. "Montana," he said a little louder. "May I come in?"

"I… I suppose so," she called back, but didn't sound too sure. He opened the door a crack and peeked around it. If she was still undressed, he didn't want anyone walking past to see. As her husband, he was the only one with that privilege. Of course, he was only her husband in name, so he had no such right either.

Oh, what a tangled web…

The phrase came to mind, but didn't appease him. How the Dickens did he end up here? Riding to Stratford was meant to be easy. Ride here, stop her traveling further, then take Montana Brown back home and keep her under his protection.

Instead, he'd encounter those vicious women. He rolled his eyes. Perhaps vicious was too harsh a word, but they were certainly unrelenting. He was determined, too. Determined to get an annulment, sooner rather than later.

Chapter Five

Colt took his time walking into their shared room. Montana had her back to him, but had a towel wrapped around the top part of her body.

She was red raw. "What have you done to yourself?" he asked as he hurried toward her.

She turned to face him and his heart broke. Tears flooded her face, and her skin was red on every part he could see.

She took a deep breath before answering. "I had to get him off me. His smell, his touch." Her voice got smaller the longer she spoke, and it was clear to Colt she was far more distressed than he'd originally thought. "I had a bath last night," she whispered. "But I could still smell him."

He didn't think twice – Colt pulled her against him, and cradled Montana in his arms. *You're an insensitive fool*, he told himself. *Why hadn't he realized she would feel that way?* Probably because he had little to do with women. His mother was a cheerful person. She'd never been harmed or traumatized her entire life. As far as Colt could tell, she'd lived a fairy-tale life until her premature death.

His wife sobbed against his chest. Crying women – he couldn't deal with them. Didn't know how to deal with them. But here he was with his arms wrapped around his wife, comforting her. At least he hoped that was what he was doing. One hand rubbed circles against her back, and the other held her tight. *Why was he doing that?* Because it was the right thing to do. He already knew the answer, but the question of why it felt so good comforting her was out of his grasp.

She swiped at her eyes and glanced up at him. "I'm sorry," she whispered. "I should splash cold water on my face. I'm a mess and need to clean up."

He frowned then. His fingers seemed to work on their own at lifting her chin to make her look at him. "You're not a mess, you're beautiful," he said. "Promise me you'll stop scrubbing your skin."

She nodded, but he wasn't convinced. "I will arrange for a hot bath. Will that help?"

She opened her mouth to speak, then slammed it shut again as though she was too frightened to speak in case the tears fell all over again. Instead, she nodded.

"Stay in here and don't unlock the door to anyone but me."

She nodded again, and he left her alone.

Climbing the stairs, Colt had time to think. Perhaps Miss Montana Brown, or Mrs. Montana Harris as she was now known, was safer as his wife. She could no longer be traced by the name she'd been known as, and she'd be in his protective care. Judge Ravin was unlikely to arrive for at least another week, and possibly longer. The fact they were married meant her reputation was not compromised, and she could hold her head high.

Those dreadful sisters might have done them both a favor. He screwed up his face. Perhaps he shouldn't go that far.

He stood outside the bathroom with his arms crossed. If he did nothing else tonight, he would ensure his wife bathed unheeded. It was the least she deserved.

"What are you doing outside the women's bathroom?" Miss Josephine demanded. He silently said several curse words. If only she knew.

"Protecting my wife."

"I need to use the bathroom." She harrumphed. Colt was convinced she used it as a weapon, except it didn't work on him.

"You'll just have to wait your turn," he said as he smiled sweetly. "I'm sure Montana won't be much longer.

She turned to leave, then suddenly spun back. "Why do you need to protect her?" She studied him then. The woman was so, so annoying.

"Ah, because she's my wife." Better to keep it to himself. Besides, it was not this old busy-body's business.

Miss Josephine looked ready to attack him. Too bad. He had no intention of telling her anything. She turned away again, just as the bathroom door opened. He stared down at Montana. She appeared far more relaxed. "Feel better?"

"You wouldn't believe the difference that bath has made." He moved to her side and put an arm around her.

"I'm glad. Time for bed," he whispered, and guided her toward their room. He heard another harrumph as they walked away. It was all Colt could do to stop from laughing.

He pulled the room key from his pocket and unlocked the door. He'd left the lantern on to ensure he could see if anyone had been there. Glancing about, it all looked as it should. The door clicked behind them as he locked it, and he was certain they would be left alone tonight. Apart from those meddling women, not a soul knew they were there. Not even his deputy.

Colt watched as Montana removed her robe. He wasn't sure what he'd expected, but a flannel nightgown wasn't one of them. She'd carefully removed the quilt, folding it, then putting it aside. Then she climbed into the freshly made bed. He heard her sigh as her head hit the pillow. "Goodnight," she whispered, and only moments later, her breathing pattern changed. His wife was already asleep.

Colt stared down at the sofa in the corner of the room. He'd found a blanket in the cupboard, along with a sad-looking pillow, and commandeered them for himself. He already knew his wedding night was going to be a miserable one, right here on the little sofa.

He sat down, removed his boots, then flipped his long legs up on the tiny excuse for a couch. It was so small it didn't even earn its name. You would barely fit two small women side by side on this thing, and Miss Josephine would be hard-pressed to sit there alone. He was practically sitting up, and it was beyond frustrating when, not five steps away, there was a warm and comfortable bed.

One with a warm body in it.

He sat up again. There was no way in Hades he could sleep there. He did what he should have done from the beginning and removed his shirt and pants. He made a small pile next to the bed, shoved his pistol underneath the pillow on the bed, and climbed under the warm and inviting bedding. Colt could feel the warmth coming from his wife. Knowing she was there for the taking was difficult, but he'd been brought up as a gentleman. He did not have permission to touch her, let alone do anything else, and he would keep his distance.

It was mighty hard, but he closed his eyes and tried to sleep. Some hours later, he finally nodded off.

The sun drifting through the curtainless windows woke him, and Colt lay there until he realized exactly where he was. He had a restless night, but the constant breathing of his wife next to him had calmed him. Colt felt a weight on him. He lifted his head gingerly to find Montana snuggled next to him with her arm across his chest. It felt good, but he wasn't sure what she would think of this turn of events.

He lay quietly watching the sun rise through the window and wondered what the day would bring. As a married man, things were different. He had more than only himself to worry about. Now he had a wife to protect. Not that they would be married long. Colt sighed. Montana seemed to be a sweet young lady. Totally innocent and caught in the middle of the madness that was Jack Tritton.

The man was a blight on society. Took whatever he wanted and had no concern about what or who he harmed in the process. Colt felt his anger rising. And that would never do. He glanced down into the face of the angel laying next to him. She snuggled even nearer, and he reveled in her closeness. He wanted to reach out and stroke her cheek, to kiss those luscious lips, but knew he had to refrain. If he didn't, Colt was certain all hell would break loose. He'd heard the high-pitched screech his wife was capable of, and had no intention of inducing it again. Especially not here in this room, in the early hours of the morning. He could just imagine the wrath he would receive from those nosey sisters. It was enough to make him cringe.

Montana's eyes fluttered open, and she stared at him. At first she seemed startled, then comprehension set it. Her gaze moved from his face to where her arm lay across his bare chest. She gasped, then pulled the bedding up to her chin. "What are you doing in my bed?" she demanded, fury clear on her face.

He chuckled, but knew it was no laughing matter. "I'm your husband," he said, trying to keep a straight face.

"I know but..." Suddenly her eyes opened wide in astonishment. "Did we...?" Terror was written all over her face now.

All thoughts of laughter left him. "My dear girl," he said steadily. "If we'd, ah, I'd like to think you would remember every moment." She pierced him with her gaze. "The sofa was far too small and I couldn't sleep. I've been here most of the night."

She gasped again.

"You didn't seem to mind. When I woke up you were snuggled into me, and your arm was across my chest. In fact, it's still there." She stared at her arm, then quickly snatched it away. He couldn't help but chuckle. Montana glared at him.

Colt noticed she was still close to him, even if she did have the bedding pulled up to cover herself. She soon remedied that. Such a shame. It felt good having her hold him like that.

"You need to get out of my bed," Montana told him firmly.

Her words puzzled him for a moment. Probably the lack of sleep. But then he realized what she was telling him. "My dear lady," he drawled. "This is as much my bed as it is yours. Why," he said, feigning disbelief, "I even paid for it. So I guess it truly is my bed." He studied her, and it was clear to Colt she didn't know what to do or say. He wanted to reassure her, but liked this cat-and-mouse game they were playing.

Montana had not looked him in the eye, not really. She would begin to speak, then turned her head away. Perhaps she thought not looking at him would make her words easier to say. He listened, but decided she was not being sincere. More than anything, she sounded conflicted. If he had to guess, Colt felt she enjoyed having him there. Perhaps she felt protected, he wasn't sure, but every time she moved away from his side, she subconsciously moved next to him again.

She certainly was a strange one. But she was also very beautiful. Even with her hair mussed and her half-asleep appearance, she was the most attractive woman he'd ever seen. Not that looks meant anything. He'd met women who could knock a man over with their beauty, but were the most vile creatures the Lord ever produced.

Not this one. She was the complete package – lovely to look at, and with a personality to bowl any man over.

Colt halted. What was he doing? He sounded like a love-sick puppy. He had been forced to marry this woman by two such nasty women, and he was thinking like this? He needed to keep in mind that Montana was also forced into the marriage. He wasn't convinced she was compliant, either. However, she didn't speak up when the preacher asked if anyone objected. Neither did he, for that matter. What was wrong with him?

"Well, my dear," he said, sliding out of the bed. "I need to get up. I want to ensure those two wicked witches, er, women, actually leave town." He watched as a sly smile played on her lips.

His stomach suddenly rumbled. "That reminds me, I didn't eat last night," he said. "It must be time for breakfast." He stood then, and Montana's eyes opened in shock, then a wide smile appeared. Colt looked down. He wore nothing but his boxers.

Chapter Six

Waving those interfering old ladies off felt good. Colt couldn't believe he'd let them coerce him into marrying a witness. Not that they knew she was a witness. As much as he'd tried to steer clear of them, the newlyweds found themselves bogged down with the pair at breakfast. It was excruciatingly painful.

At least they were gone now, and he'd been there to ensure that had happened. He turned to his wife. "Now it's our turn to leave. I'll fetch Nellie from the livery, with the buggy, of course, and we'll make our way home."

She looked stricken. "We can't go yet. The preacher needs to cancel our marriage."

Cancel their marriage? What was she talking about? "My dear wife," he said, emphasizing the wife part, "the preacher doesn't have to power to do that. Only a judge can annul a marriage."

She went deathly white. "Can't he just remove our listing from the register? We can tear up the marriage certificate while he's there, and…"

"Nope." She was far more naïve than he'd first thought. "There's a process. Only a judge can do all that. The reason must be valid. I'm not even certain we have a convincing reason."

Her shoulders slumped, and Montana looked on the verge of tears. "Well, I'm going to see the preacher, anyway." She stomped away then, and Colt had no choice but to follow.

As they sat inside the warm house, the preacher explained exactly what Colt had already told Montana. "But we were forced," she wailed.

"I'm sorry, my dear. You didn't look pressured nor did you speak up. Neither did the marshal. It is all perfectly legal."

"We'll see the judge. I'm sure he can fix it," Colt explained. "Montana thought it would be an easy fix, but we both know it's not." He shook the preacher's hand.

"Mrs. Harris," the preacher said gently. "You may come to love each other. Don't discount it."

"Love? I barely know this man. I cannot see myself loving him." She turned to Colt then. "No offense meant."

"None taken," he said. If he was honest with himself, he did take offense. He'd put his life on the line for this ungrateful woman, and that's how she treated him? Well, if an annulment was what she wanted, it was exactly what she would get.

When Judge Ravin arrived, hopefully in the next few days, Colt would make it a priority to have their marriage annulled. He should have stood his ground with the sisters and refused to marry Miss Montana Brown. He was wrong in his original assessment. She might be lovely, but she was a viper, just like those dreadful sisters, and he should have fought them far more forcefully.

The trip back to Harrigan's Pass was in near silence. She acted like their situation was his fault. It totally wasn't. All she had to do was say no. Or tell the preacher she was being coerced by those evil women. Only she didn't, and Colt wondered if she had some sort of motive. If she thought she was marrying someone rich, she was wrong. If she thought he lived in a mansion, she was also wrong.

As marshal, he had a small dwelling behind the jailhouse. It came with the job, and it wasn't much to look at. It would accommodate a wife, but he doubted she would tolerate it for long. Montana seemed like a person who was used to the good life.

Colt did not know why he'd come to that conclusion. He glanced across at her. Her clothes were not cheap, off the rack clothes. She also held herself in a way that screamed money. When she let her guard down, he saw a different side to her, but that was rare. He liked that side of her far better.

He glanced across at her momentarily. Montana gave him the cold shoulder for most of the way back home. She rarely spoke, except to say she was hungry or needed to use the privy. It was a long ride, and he couldn't deny her that. "We'll be at Harlington soon. Do you want to stop? We still have a few hours of travel."

She glared at him. "Of course." Montana pursed her lips and straightened her shoulders. He was so glad he'd brought the buggy along, otherwise they'd be doing this trip shoved up together on Nellie. It would have meant an additional overnight stay, as he wouldn't push his horse that much. He didn't relish with the way she was behaving and it would have been intolerable with the two of them on one horse.

"None of this is my fault," he said briskly, and let his words hang it the air.

She turned and stared at him. "Nor mine." She was as determined as he was. Truth be told, neither of them was to blame.

A short time later, they arrived at the tiny town called Harlington. He hadn't stopped here on his way to collect Montana, as he was in a rush to get her. Nellie was flailing, and that wouldn't do. He glanced about, noticing the livery down the road. At the other end of town stood a small hotel. There was a diner opposite. "We're staying the night," he announced.

"No," Montana said. "I refuse." Her lips were pursed and her eyes pierced him. She sure was cantankerous when she wanted to be. Probably learned that from those terrible sisters.

He looked down at her. His wife, who didn't even reach his shoulders, was being defiant. "Too bad," he said. "Nellie needs a break. She's not used to this sort of travel, and I won't push her further." He flicked the reins, and they headed toward the livery. "I'll book her in for the night, and we'll get a room somewhere." He would not argue. His word was final.

"I'm not staying," she said, but Colt ignored her. "Did you hear me?"

He turned to her then. "Stop being a thorn in my side. Nellie's wellbeing is far more important than anything you might want." She was acting like a spoiled brat. It was the sort of behavior you would expect from a rich kid. Colt studied her. He didn't think she was rich exactly, but there were signs that didn't add up. "This fiancée, what was his upbringing?"

She paled. Pursing her lips again, she finally answered. "I don't want to talk about him, and I won't," she said firmly. He found her words strange.

When they arrived at the livery, Colt climbed down from the buggy. "You stay here," he commanded, then headed to the livery office. He arranged for Nellie to be looked after and left her in the hands of the owner.

Montana still sat on the buggy when he returned. He lifted her down, his hands around her waist. She stared into his face as he put her to the ground. The woman seemed to possess some sort of witchcraft – it mesmerized him just staring into her face. "Nellie is in excellent hands," he said, running a gentle hand down the mare's neck. "We'll see you tomorrow," he told her as they walked away. He snatched up their few belongings and headed for the hotel.

"Aren't getting something to eat?" she complained.

Colt rolled his eyes. "Of course we are. We'll arrange a room and I can leave our bags there instead of carting them around town."

"Oh." Heat flooded her face. He wasn't sure if she was panicking about stopping here for a reason known only to Montana, or whether she was simply being difficult.

He glanced around the lobby of the Harlington Hotel. It looked far nicer than the one at Stratford. "My wife and I need a room for the night," he told the clerk. Colt handed over the fee and was handed a key.

"Thank you, Marshal," the clerk said. "Good day to you, Mrs. Harris." Montana startled at the use of her married name. She wouldn't get used to it before it was no longer hers. Colt was certain of that. Only a few more days, by his reckoning.

They headed upstairs. Colt opened the door, but dropped their bags inside the door, then stepped back. Montana stared at him. "What are you doing?" she asked, confusion written all over her face.

He chuckled. "What I should have done last night. There may not be another chance for either of us." Colt leaned down and picked her up. She was light as a feather. "I'm carrying you across the threshold. It's not our home, but it will have to do."

He expected her to kick and scream and carry on, but she didn't. Instead, she smiled. Pink flooded her cheeks, and she leaned her head against his chest. Was Montana playing a part, or was she beginning to like him? It surely wasn't the latter.

Her hands slid up and around his neck, and Colt's heart pounded. Surely she wasn't going to… Before he could finish the thought, she kissed him.

It wasn't a brief peck on the cheek, but a full-on kiss, right on his lips. At first, he floundered. Colt wasn't prepared for that. Shouldn't he be the one to instigate such a thing? He was the man, after all. Her hands ran through his hair and down his face. Now his heart fluttered. This time, he instigated the kiss.

He suddenly pulled back. What was he doing? They would get an annulment in a few days. Until then, they needed to keep their distance, to talk only when they needed to talk, and have little to do with each other.

Only that would be difficult, since he was here as her protector. But he was also her husband. He could easily take on that role permanently. At least if she wasn't so ornery.

He stared into Montana's face and stared. She was grinning.

She was playing him. There was no doubt in his mind. "Why'd you do that?" He wiped his hand across his mouth. He needed to wipe away the feel of her soft lips.

She shrugged her shoulders. "Why not?" She apparently saw no issue in playing with him.

Colt did, and he wouldn't forgive her for it.

He suddenly put her to the floor, and Montana seemed annoyed. "Don't play games," he said, then picked up their luggage and placed it on the other side of the room. Montana sat on the side of the bed. He watched as she glanced about. This room was smaller than the previous hotel, and there was no sofa. That meant no argument about where he slept tonight.

She studied him but said nothing. "We should find somewhere to eat," he said, trying to break the awkward silence. Besides, he was hungry.

"I need to freshen up first." She played with her hair as if trying to prove a point.

Colt accompanied her to the bathroom, where he waited outside. Why was it each time he did that, other women needed to use the bathroom and gave him weird looks? "Waiting for my wife," he said casually, as if every husband stood guarding the bathroom while their wives were inside. "She won't be long," he added.

Almost at that very moment, Montana emerged from the room. She looked far fresher than she had when she went in, and had a smile on her face. "I'm ready now," she said, then turned to the other woman. "I apologize for holding you up. Long trip," she explained.

"It is perfectly alright, my dear." She smiled and went into the bathroom. Colt slipped an arm up around her and they soon headed out.

"We could eat here at the hotel, but I think the diner will be better," Colt said as they went down the stairs from their room.

Montana gazed up at him with those beautiful brown eyes. They got him every time. "The diner sounds good," she said, then reached for his hand. Colt flinched. He wasn't sure if she was still playing with him, or trying to give the appearance of a married couple. He unlinked their hands, then hooked her arm through his. He felt far more comfortable that way. Holding hands, to him, gave the feeling of intimacy. They were far from that in their phony marriage.

They left the hotel and went over the road to the diner. It was far from full, but the customers seemed to be satisfied with their food. "Welcome!" An older woman greeted them at the door. "Table for two?"

"Yes, thank you," Colt said, then the woman guided them to their table.

"Passing through, or settling in Harlington?"

"We're passing through. On our way home to Harrigan's Pass," he said.

"We just got married," Montana said, smiling. "Yesterday." Her eyes opened wide in excitement, as though they were truly married. Well, yes, they were married, but not in the true sense. Colt wasn't sure why she thought it appropriate to tell this complete stranger.

The woman clapped her hands together. "Newlyweds! Oooh, congratulations," she said, excitement overtaking her. "Here's the menu," she said, handing each of them one. "Today's special is Chicken Pot Pie, and," she turned to Colt, "we also have steak and veg. Men seem to prefer that."

"I'll have the steak and veg," Colt told her. "What about you, my darling?" Since Montana was being precious about the whole marriage thing, he'd play it up too.

"Chicken Pot Pie, please. May I have a glass of lemonade with mine?"

"Of course. Coffee for you, Marshal, or would you prefer lemonade too?" A smile played on her lips, and he knew their server was having a joke with him.

"Coffee, please." She left them then, and he turned to Montana. "What was that about? Why did you tell her we were newlyweds?"

She fluttered her eyelashes at him. "Because we are."

Darn it, she was playing with him again. One minute she didn't want to be married, the next minute she did. He did not want to be married to this woman. She was outright weird. Hot one minute, cold the next.

He had no intention of staying married to someone as crazy as Montana Brown. His hands were on the table as he waited for their food to arrive. Without warning, Montana slid her hand across the table and covered one of his. He glared at her. "Why did you do that? Honestly, Montana, I cannot fathom you."

"I… I'm scared, that's all," she whispered. "What if the judge won't give us an annulment? What happens then?"

Colt hadn't thought of that possibility. "Am I really that bad?"

"You're not," she whispered. "And that's the problem."

Colt didn't have the chance to answer as their food arrived. But it got him wondering – what was going on in that pretty little head of his pretend wife?

Chapter Seven

Colt woke up the next morning the same way he had the day before – with his wife snuggled into him, and her arm across his bare chest. He certainly wouldn't complain about it, nor would he grumble about gazing into that sweet face each morning.

Her hair lay across the pillow, and he wanted nothing more than to run his fingers through it, but he didn't dare. Her lips were slightly open, and ripe for kissing, but having his face slapped was not the best way to start the day.

His thoughts made Colt chuckle. But only momentarily. What if their marriage was real? Things would be very different between them. This cat-and-mouse game Montana was playing would disappear. When she kissed him, he would enjoy it, not get annoyed with her.

He closed his eyes and tried to push his ridiculous theories aside. He was doing this to protect Montana. There was no other reason. Few marshals or other lawman married, and there was a good reason for that. Many of them ended up dead, or put their wives in danger. Apart from the fact Montana didn't want to be married to him, he was supposed to be protecting her, not putting her in further danger.

What was he thinking?

She stirred. Her lips opened, and she gasped. "Good morning, wife," he said, chuckling at his own joke.

Instead of answering, she harrumphed. Not a good sign. Did that mean she would turn into a Josephine Ranwell? At least he wouldn't be around to find out. "Get dressed," he said briskly. "We have time for breakfast, and then we'll leave." He sat on the side of the bed for a brief time, then stood. Wearing only his boxers, he strolled across the room to retrieve his clothes and his gun belt. He heard Montana gasp at his near nakedness and grinned. She should be used to it by now – it was the second time she'd seen him this way.

If they were married, she would see it daily. Only he usually didn't wear the boxers. He only wore them out of respect for her.

He pulled on his pants, then retrieved a clean shirt out of his bag and put that on. Last, he added his gun belt.

"Do you really need to wear that thing?" He wasn't aware she was watching him dress until that moment.

"I do. Why are you watching me dress? That's a bit... creepy, don't you think?"

She glared at him. "We're married!" She harrumphed again, then climbed out of the bed. Her flannel nightgown left everything to the imagination, more's the pity. If they were truly married, he would burn that thing and buy a nightgown that was a little more revealing.

Colt shook his head. What was wrong with him? He shouldn't be having such thoughts. Protect Montana, protect Montana. He said the mantra over and over in his head. Hopefully, doing so would take his mind off the woman and put it back on the job at hand.

"Please leave," she demanded.

Colt spun around to face her. "What?" He did not know what she was talking about.

"I need to dress, and I'm not doing that with you in the room." She held up her undergarments then, obviously to shock him, and Colt couldn't get out of there quick enough.

Would he ever get over the embarrassment? "I'll be right outside," he said, then hurried out of the room.

He could hear her moving about, but didn't dare go inside. Several women went past on the way to the bathroom and gave him an odd look. "Waiting for my wife," he said as he nodded, and they continued on their way. The fact she was a fake wife and didn't want him to see her dress was another matter entirely.

Colt knew he should have been more sensitive to her feelings. Being a single woman, she would never have seen a man without his clothes. As much as he thought it funny to walk around in only his boxers, it really wasn't. He needed to be more attuned to her needs. The trouble was, apart from his mother, Colt hadn't spent much time with women.

His job entailed working more with men than women, and the few he'd encountered tended to be soiled doves. They were a whole different breed of women.

Montana was more genteel and appeared to be very naïve. He had to remember that. The door clicked, then his wife came out to meet him. "Ready?"

She nodded. "What should I do with my things?"

He glanced down. The overnight bag was in her hands. "Leave it there. We'll collection our bags after breakfast. We won't be hanging around long."

They ate at the hotel. Breakfast was included in the cost, so they might as well avail themselves. Montana was silent during the meal and had a sadness about her. "What are you thinking about?"

Her sad eyes glanced up at him. "Nothing. Everything."

Colt frowned. "That's a strange thing to say."

"My life is nothing. I'm not important to anyone. That's the nothing part." His heart sank. Why would she think that? Before he had a chance to speak, she continued. "Everything has gone wrong in the past week. My life has been turned upside down. To top it all off, I was forced to marry a man I don't know, and who hates me."

Her eyes filled with tears, but she fought them back. *What could he do to fix this?* "I don't hate you. I promise I don't." He leaned across the table to stop busy-bodies from hearing. "We're both in the same situation," he whispered. "Neither of us wanted to get married. We'll fix it when Judge Ravin arrives." He sat back then, proud he'd fixed all her problems.

"What if he refuses to help us? What then?"

Colt was shaken to his core. What then, indeed?

Montana breathed a sigh of relief when they finally pulled into Harrigan's Pass. It had been a long few days, and he was equally happy to be back home as Montana was. Although she could hardly call it home. She'd spent one night there, and from all accounts, it wasn't even an entire night. She'd snuck out in the early hours to catch the stagecoach out of town.

They pulled into the livery, and he helped Montana down from the buggy. "I'll take it from here, Marshal. You and the young lady look clean puckered out."

"Thanks, Jack. Much appreciated. It will be good to get back into my own bed." Montana might not think so. He hadn't breached the subject yet, but was certain she planned on going back to Miss Mae's. That wasn't an option. Not while he was meant to protect her.

They walked across to the Marshal's Office, Colt carrying both their bags. "Finally!" his deputy said. "I was beginning to worry. Look at this," he said, handing Colt a telegraph.

Colt studied it. The news wasn't good. "When did this arrive?" he demanded.

His deputy glanced across at Montana, then back to Colt. "Yesterday. What are you going to do about it?"

"What they sent me to do. Protect my wife." The words slipped out. He hadn't meant to disclose *that* information to his deputy.

"Wife? Are you crazy in the head?"

"It's a long story, Edgar. I'm too tired to tell it now." He slapped the telegraph onto his desk, then headed to his private quarters. "I'll be back when I'm ready," he said firmly, then took Montana to her new home.

"What is this?" she asked, glancing around the small cabin that sat behind the Marshal's Office.

He took a deep breath. Colt knew it wouldn't go over well and hoped she could hold her temper. "This is our home." He watched her closely for signs of an explosion. None came.

"What about Miss Mae's? I liked it there."

"You liked it so much you ran away. No, you won't be going back there. You are my wife, and will live here with me. Besides, I can't protect you if you're living in another building. Especially one across town." The moment he spoke the words, Colt knew he'd said the wrong thing.

"Does that mean if I find somewhere closer, I can stay there?" He could see what she was doing, but it wouldn't work.

"Definitely not. You will stay here with me. It's not negotiable."

She screwed up her face at him, then strolled through his cottage. Technically, it was now their cottage. He needed to remember that.

She went into the kitchen, but said nothing. Then Montana studied his bedroom. Their bedroom, and sat on the side of the bed. She gave a little bounce, just as she'd done in each of the hotels. She said nothing, but moved further along. "Where's the second bed?" she asked, glancing about the spare room.

"There is none, as you can see. That room is traditionally used for storage. It's rare for marshals to marry, and only the main bedroom is used."

She straightened her shoulders, and Colt could see she was itching for a fight. "The room is near empty. You could get another bed."

He could but he wasn't going to. "It's only short term, and I'm not going to the expense. Besides, I can better protect you if we're in the same bed."

She turned away from him without uttering another word. Montana continued her tour of the cottage and stopped at the outdated bathroom. "At least there's an inside bathroom," she said. Montana was clearly not happy, but the unfortunate fact was there was nothing Colt could do about it. "What was the telegraph about?" She pierced him with her gaze then. It was as if she knew the message affected her.

"Nothing for you to worry about." Except it was.

"I don't believe you," Montana said firmly. "Tell me what was in it."

Colt weighed his words. "There are still gang members at large. We thought we had them all." Montana looked ready to drop. Colt stepped forward and wrapped his arms around her – as much for himself as it was for her. "I promise I will keep you safe." He lifted her chin with his fingers and gazed down into those beautiful brown eyes. "Now you see why I need you to stay here."

She nodded, then tucked her head against him again.

Every time he held her, Colt lost a little more of his heart. How long Montana would live in his cottage, sleep in his bed, he didn't know. He also didn't know how long it would take for him to completely lose his heart to her.

Chapter Eight

Waking up in Colt's cottage felt like coming home.

Montana didn't know why. She only knew it felt as though she'd lived there forever. She was certain it wasn't the building itself, it was totally foreign to her. It wasn't the bed either, it was her first time sleeping here. *Was it because of the man whose arms she was wrapped in? The man she didn't want to marry, but now felt an affinity to?* She decided it had to be.

There was a barrier between them, and she knew exactly what it was – she was hiding the truth from him.

They might be pretending to be married, and she might fight his every decision, but she had feelings for Marshal Colt Harris. Perhaps if things were different, she may even let herself fall for the man.

Montana shook her head. What a ridiculous thing to think. The moment the danger was over, and as soon as the trial was done, he would dump her as quickly as he could. There was one reason, and one reason only he kept her close, and that was because of those gang members still at large.

She couldn't believe it – she'd gone from one horrific situation to another. When she closed her eyes, she still saw that awful man. Montana closed her eyes from the memory, but his disgusting face flashed in front of her. If it wasn't for Colt, she did not know where she would be now.

Probably dead at the bottom of a cliff where no one would find her.

"Are you alright?" Colt whispered. His voice was so quiet she wasn't startled, nor was she scared. His presence made her feel so much better. Safer.

She shook her head. "Bad memories," she whispered back. Without another word, he pulled her close and wrapped her in his arms.

Colt was a good man. She could see that now. He had protected her from the very start. He'd married her when it seemed there was no other choice, and he hadn't laid a finger on her. Oh, he could have demanded his husbandly rights, but not once did he do that. He had kissed her, but only after Montana had kissed him first. She blamed herself for his reaction. What man is going to resist a woman who is so blatantly throwing herself at him?

She didn't even know why she did it. On some deeper level, Montana wondered if she was trying to force him to claim her as his own. After all she'd been through lately, it was time for something good to happen in her life. Colt could be her something good.

He continued to hold her, his breath warm on her cheek. "I won't let you go," he whispered. "I'll protect you."

She knew he would. But was it only protection she wanted? Montana knew she wanted so much more, but that wasn't what Colt was offering. One of these days, hopefully not in the too distant future, she would find a man who wanted her for herself. Someone who would love and protect her because they loved her, not because they were being paid to shield her from criminals. In less than a week, she'd been put in two precarious situations. In both cases, she'd been saved. She thought she loved Lester, and he love her. Montana couldn't have been more wrong. Life was repeating itself, and it was breaking her heart.

She let herself relax in Colt's arms, knowing he was there for her. She just wished he had even a hint of feelings for her.

Montana didn't know how much later she awoke, but Colt was gone. His side of the bed was stone cold, telling her he'd been up a while. The sun shone through the thin curtains of the bedroom, and she closed her eyes against it.

She heard a noise coming from another part of the house and figured Colt was making himself coffee.

"Good morning, sleepyhead," he said as he walked into the bedroom. He was carrying a tray, and the aroma was enticing. "Sit up and have your breakfast." He sat the tray on her lap when she was upright, then sat on the side of the bed.

Montana leaned in and breathed in the wonderful aroma. "You made this?" She laughed then because she figured he probably bought it from the diner. She quickly realized he wouldn't have left her alone and unprotected.

"I can cook, you know," he said, then chuckled. "A man would starve otherwise."

She took a mouthful of the scrambled eggs. "This is delicious," she said when her mouth was empty. "Have you eaten yet?"

"I have. You eat up. Stay in bed as long as you like. We're not going anywhere."

Just as she figured. He wasn't letting her out of the house. Still, it was cozy here, and she had everything she needed. A bed to sleep in, a kitchen to cook in, and a man to keep close.

She almost choked on her food. Where did that last thought come from? Montana had one goal, and one goal only – get through this, then arrange their annulment. She was certain Colt would want the same.

He was a bachelor with no ties, and a job that put him in constant danger. He'd said it himself – most marshals did not marry because of the danger that came with their work. It was then it hit her. Did protecting her put him in an even more dangerous situation? This time, she choked. The last thing Montana wanted was to have Colt's life in danger because of her. Somehow, she had to rectify the situation. She had to get away from Harrigan's Pass and break all ties with Colt. How did she do that and still get their marriage annulled? Surely it wasn't impossible?

Colt hurried into the bedroom. He pushed the tray aside and thumped her on the back. Tears ran down her face, not because she was choking, but because she knew she had to leave him.

Finally, the lump of food came flying out of her mouth. He wiped her tears away. "It's alright now," he said, and pulled her against his chest. He was ghostly white. She'd caused that. Maybe it would have been better if she had choked. It would have ended both their problems. She would not be a burden, she'd be out of his life, and he would be free to marry someone he loved.

His hands ran circles over her back. Colt's touch was comforting. She'd never felt this strongly about

Lester, and she'd known him far longer than she'd know Colt. She'd been engaged to Lester for nearly a year, but her heart didn't flutter when he came into the room. Shivers didn't run down her spine when he touched her. And she didn't crave his presence when he wasn't around.

But she did with Colt.

She wasn't sure when it had happened, but Montana's arms were up around his back. She suddenly pulled back and stared up into his face. His eyes were the brightest blue she'd ever seen, and his brown hair had a kink to it that sent it flying over his eyes. He needed a decent hair cut to fix it.

Without her permission, her hand went up and caressed his cheek. Tingles went through her fingers. He stared at her, his eyes big and round in astonishment. "What are you doing?" he demanded. Colt was cross with her. That was probably a good thing.

What did she say? Showing you how much I've grown to love you? That would never do. Instead, she said. "I'm sorry. I got a bit carried away."

He merely nodded, then stood at the knock on the door. Without another word, he left her alone.

Montana heard mutterings at the door, then the door slammed shut. Colt had a telegraph in his hand.

"Judge Ravin has taken ill. They're sending Judge Claremont instead." He looked far from happy.

"Is that a problem?"

"Not for the prisoners. They'll be jailed either way. For us, for our marriage… it could be." He sighed. "Judge Claremont is not one to care much for people. He only wants to get the job done and move onto the next town." Colt ran his fingers through his already mussed hair. "I don't know if he'll grant our annulment."

Montana's heart thudded. Her mind was now made up. She had to leave town, and quickly. The train went through Harrigan's Pass twice a week, and she knew the time because she'd been on the train a few days ago. By her reckoning, it should come through again later today. All she had to do was get to the train station without Colt knowing she'd gone.

Chapter Nine

Colt woke up with a start.

Montana said she needed to rest. There was nothing else to do in his cottage, so he laid down with her. It was mid-afternoon; he had not thought he would fall asleep, but that was exactly what he'd done.

She wasn't in bed, and the sheets were cold. She wasn't foolish enough to leave the cottage, so she had to be here somewhere. Perhaps she was cooking. He listened, but heard no movement. He hurried out of bed and went to the kitchen. Montana wasn't there, and there was no sigh she had cooked anything.

He checked the bathroom. She wasn't there either. He ran back to the bedroom and checked the wardrobe. Her few belongings were gone. His heart pounded. Why would she be so incredibly foolish to leave his cottage, knowing her life was in danger? Was it related to Judge Ravin not coming?

He took a huge breath and let it out slowly. That had to be it. Until he'd told her that information, she seemed reasonably content. After that she was edgy, couldn't keep still. She acted differently to the way she had before.

Colt's head was pounding. If the gang found her, she was dead. He had no doubt about it. There was only one way out of town, and that was via the train. He checked the time. Five minutes before the next train arrived. He might make it if he rushed. He grabbed his hat and ran to the train station., collecting Edgar, his deputy, on the way. He could hear the whistle in the distance. His chest hurt from running so fast, but he wouldn't stop.

Whatever Montana had been thinking, he had no idea. Her life was on the line every moment she was out in public. It made sense for the rest of the Tritton gang to assume she was still in town. His heart hurt when realization hit – she could already lay dead on that filthy train platform.

Colt's first instinct was to protect her. That was always his job. But this was about more than what he had to do. This was about loving the woman he'd married. Until now, he'd refused to admit it. Now that her life was on the line, he had no choice but to be honest with himself. And her.

What would Montana think of all this? He swallowed back the emotion that was heavy in his chest.

Finally, finally! Colt arrived at the train station. Outside he leaned over and took a moment to catch his breath – he was no use to Montana if he couldn't breathe. His gun hand needed to be steady. At the same time, he hoped he didn't need it.

He used the time to pray. "Lord," he whispered. "I know I'm not worthy, but can you please spare Montana? She's a good person, but has been dealt a harsh hand, and not of her own doing." He gazed heavenward. "Lord, you probably already know, but I've fallen in love with her. I want to grow old with her." His own words choked him up. It was one of the few times in his life Colt had felt so emotional.

Finally, he had caught his breath. Was that God's doing? He wasn't sure.

As he straightened, Edgar caught up with him.

The pair glanced about. The place didn't look any different from normal. Couples strolled across the station on their way to buy tickets, and children ran in front of them. Nothing seemed out of place.

The train whistle got closer. The train was almost there. "We'll have to check the platform," Colt said, knowing it was the last place he wanted to encounter gang members. There would be too many people waiting there for his liking, not to mention plenty of places for them to hide in. Like the stationmaster's office.

Colt carefully made his way onto the platform. Passengers glanced up and saw the marshal and his deputy, guns in hand, and looked up in shock. Colt put his fingers to his lips and waved them off the platform. They went without a word.

Smoke filled the platform as the train arrived. Apart from the sound of the train, it was deathly quiet. Too quiet for Colt's liking. Where was Montana?

He stayed back, out of sight. Perhaps if the gang didn't know he was there, they might show themselves and make their move. He used that time to calm himself. His heart pounded so loud it sounded like drums in his ears. The pounding slowed, but didn't disappear.

Colt scoured the platform with his eyes. It was a continuous motion. There was nothing to see. If that was the case, where was Montana? There was no other way out of Harrigan's Pass, so this was the obvious place for her to go.

Edgar tapped his arm. "There," he whispered, and pointed toward the waiting room. How he'd missed it before, Colt didn't know. "Your missus moved slightly forward. Likely on purpose," he continued in a low voice.

The train was almost upon the station and gave the whistle a long blast. There was even more smoke than before. It was difficult to see anything in front of them, and now Montana was out of sight. As if she knew, she let out a small squeal.

"Shut your mouth," a male voice said, and Colt imagined a gun in her back.

Totally ignoring her assailant, Montana squealed again. Then he heard a scuffle.

The voice was further away, and reality struck. They were not going to shoot her. The intention was to push her in front of the train. Only they hadn't factored all the smoke and coal dust into their plans.

Nor had they figured on Colt and Edgar being there.

Montana squealed again. *Good girl*, he told her mentally. *Keep doing that*. As if she'd heard, she squealed over and over until Colt was standing next to the pair.

Being this close, he could see their silhouette. He grabbed at Montana and pulled her behind him, shoving the man to the ground. It was then he noticed the second man. Edgar took care of him. The fallen man was all his, and Colt intended to ensure he didn't hurt another person anytime soon. As the assailant tried to get to his feet, Colt landed a punch on his jaw. He rolled the man over and cuffed him.

"You can join the rest of your gang," he said, pulling the man roughly to his feet, then shoving him forward.

Edgar sat both men on a nearby seat. "Do not move," he commanded. "I will shoot if you do. Have no doubt."

Colt knew he would. He put his gun away and pulled Montana close, wrapping his arms around her. *Thank you, Lord, for saving her.* Colt had prayed more today than he had for a long time. "Are you alright?" Of course she wasn't. What a stupid thing to say. "This is all my fault," he began, but she interrupted.

"No, it's my fault. I'm the one who ran."

He put his fingers to her lips. "I have something to tell you." He glanced about. "But not here. And not with these…" He shook his head. "Not here." He leaned in and kissed her forehead.

He wanted so badly to say the words, but would like the moment to be special. He also didn't want an audience, or for the place he told her to be filled with smoke and dust. It would have to wait.

With the remaining gang members rounded up and now in jail, it was safe for Montana to be alone. She desperately wanted a bath. Said she felt dirty. Colt figured that was more to do with being man-handled than from the smoke and coal dust.

She was in his cottage bathing while he and Edgar processed the two additional prisoners. As he pulled the forms out of the drawer to charge the two, he came across the annulment papers. He stared at them, then swallowed. It seemed like forever ago when they'd filled out that form. So much had happened in the interim. No longer did he want an annulment. All he wanted now was to stay married to Montana. She'd become an integral part of his life, and he couldn't imagine living the rest of his days without her.

The truth was, she didn't feel the same way. Once the trial was over, she would leave town and head to wherever it was she was going when Jack Tritton snatched her off the train.

"Marshal? Did you hear me?" Edgar's voice cut right through his heart. "I asked what you want them charged with." He stared at Colt then, as if he knew his heart was in turmoil.

"Kidnap, attempted murder, endangerment. If we hadn't cleared that platform, who knows how many people would have been killed." He ran a hand through his hair. "I'm sure I'll think of a few other charges."

A slow smiled crossed Edgar's face. "I'm always willing to help," he said, then shoved the prisoners toward the cells.

Colt pulled the annulment papers out of the drawer. He wanted to tear it up right here and now, but knew Montana was determined not to be married to him.

Montana. That sweet woman he'd fallen in love with. He needed to tell her how he felt, but would she run again? Especially knowing she already wanted to leave town.

There was only one thing for it. He had to talk to her. His mother always told him there was only one way to solve problems in a marriage, and that was to talk about it. How he wished his beautiful mother was here now – she would tell him what to do. He missed her more than he ever thought possible.

Colt shoved his hat on his head. "I'm going home," he said as Edgar returned to the office. Without another word, he left to speak with his wife.

Chapter Ten

He lightly tapped on the door before entering the cottage. For all he knew, Montana could still be in the bath. The last thing he wanted was to embarrass her. "I'm home," he called out, ensuring she knew he was there.

Total silence.

His heart skipped a beat. Colt hoped that meant she didn't hear him. He went to the bathroom and listened at the door. Not a sound. He tapped, but got no answer.

Colt slowly opened the door. His heart was hollow. It was apparent she had left. With the danger over, perhaps she thought it was time to move on. Only he didn't want her to move on. He wanted Montana to stay. But only if that was what she wanted too.

With no other trains leaving today, there was only one other place he could think of where she would go. Miss Mae's Boarding House.

He headed there immediately.

Every step of the way, his heart pounded. He was almost as scared now as he was arriving at the train station. *What was Montana thinking? Would she even talk to him?* For all he knew, Mae might not let him through the door.

"It's me again, Lord. I know I'm asking a lot of you today, and I'm sorry. I'm not usually so demanding. Can you try to get Montana to talk to me? Even if she doesn't talk, but listens. That would work." He glanced heavenward for the second time that day. "Thank you, Lord."

He pounded his fist on the door. Colt didn't mean to knock so hard, but he couldn't take it back.

Miss Mae answered. Her eyes ran from his head to his toes. "You're grubby," she said. "I heard what happened. Guess you better come in."

His heart fluttered. Montana was there. Now to get her to listen.

Miss Mae ushered him into the kitchen. "I've just taken a batch of oat cookies out of the oven. They'll be cool enough to eat soon. Coffee is ready, so sit yourself down and I'll get you some."

That was typical of Miss Mae. She loved to dish out orders. Most folks listened, and he was one of them. Especially when it came to her cooking.

"Montana is laying down. She had a hot bath, then retreated to her room." She sat a mug of coffee on the table in front of him. "That girl is deeply traumatized. She needs a good man to help fix her."

She eyed Colt then, glaring at him. "Are you that man?"

"I…" he floundered then. It wasn't a question he expected, especially from Miss Mae. He lifted the mug and gulped it down, almost choking. When he recovered, Colt straightened his shoulders. "I am," he said firmly, not taking his eyes off her.

Miss Mae smiled then. "I thought you might be."

Colt heard a door open, and a short time later, Montana entered the kitchen. Her hair was a little mussed, like she'd just woken from a nap, which was exactly what she'd done. He recalled waking up next to her these past mornings, and how good it had made him feel. Wrapping her in his arms each morning, and any other time he thought it appropriate, was something he looked forward to each day.

Why he hadn't told her how he felt, Colt didn't know, but it was time. He loved her with all his heart, and she didn't have a clue. He pushed back his chair and stood as she entered the room. Colt wanted nothing more than to rush across the kitchen and encase her in his arms. He could see she'd been crying, and it broke his heart.

Montana glanced up at him. She seemed to be startled by his presence. "Hello," she said. Miss Mae ushered her into a chair, then put a mug of tea in front of her. She sipped her tea as though she was considering her words. "What are you doing here?" she asked, glaring at him as she spoke.

His heart thudded. She hated him. It cut him in two, because if she hated him, there was no way Montana would stay married to him. "I came to talk to you." She glared again. "You only have to listen," he quickly added. "Can we move into the sitting room?" He glanced at Montana, but it was Miss Mae who answered.

"Not in those filthy clothes you can't." Her words were firm and there was no arguing.

She was right. His uniform was filthy. The train had seen to that. He nodded in her direction. "I totally understand." He stood to leave, but Miss Mae stopped him.

"You can have the kitchen, or you could take a stroll?"

He glanced across at Montana. Colt would agree to whatever she wanted. She was far more important than he was.

"I could do with a bit of fresh air," she said, then stood. "I need to fix my hair first."

Colt stared at her. "Your hair is perfect. You are beautiful. When you wake up in the morning with your hair mussed and sleep still on your face, you're beautiful. When you're asleep, you're beautiful. And with smoke and coal dust covering you, you're still beautiful." He felt Miss Mae's eyes on him, but resisted the urge to face her.

He guided Montana out of the kitchen, and she reached for her coat as they left. Colt helped her into it, and they went outside. She took a deep, fortifying breath, then let it out slowly. "I love it here in Harrigan's Pass," she whispered. "Unless there are criminals around." She turned to face him then. "Does that happen often?"

He studied her. Her chin quivered. Colt wanted to wrap her up in his warmth and assure her she was safe with him. But he'd told her that before, and look where that got her. "It doesn't. This is an anomaly. The most we usually have is a drunk here and there, and maybe a bar fight. I lock up far more drunks than anyone else." She stared at him, then nodded. "Of course I can't promise you that," he said as they strolled along the boardwalk.

"I guess not," Montana said. She slipped her arm through his. "Miss Mae has a wonderful bath," she said out of the blue.

Colt stared at her. "What?" He shook his head then, apparently missing her meaning.

She smiled briefly. "Your bath is small and old. I don't know how a person is meant to soak in it."

He frowned then. "I never use it." He glanced down. "Can you imagine these long legs fitting into that small bath?"

She laughed then. It was one of the few times Colt had seen her laugh. He liked it. He liked the way her face relaxed when she laughed, and the way her eyes crinkled up. Best of all, he liked her smile.

Suddenly, she stopped laughing. "You're missing the point," she said, then licked her lips. "You said you wanted to talk to me." She closed her eyes briefly then, and he could see she was bracing herself for the inevitable.

"It's about our annulment," he said slowly. She swallowed, then nodded, waiting for him to finish.

"The judge is here?" she asked, seemingly confused.

"He's not. Can we sit down over here?" They'd arrived at the park on the edge of town, and he guided her onto the wooden bench. It was a pleasant area, and he often sat there if he needed to think. The bench was surrounded by bushes as tall as his waist, and in front of those were a variety of flowers.

"The flowers are beautiful." Montana leaned down and breathed in the fragrance of them. "They smell nice," she said.

Enough beating around the bush. Colt needed to tell her before he backed out. "I brought you here for a reason," he said carefully, and she flinched. "It's not bad. At least I don't think it is." He reached for her hand. "I love you, Montana. I know I should have told you how I felt before this. I don't want an annulment." He gazed down into her face, but instead of the joy he'd expected to see, she was terrified.

"We can't stay married," she said miserably. "It's not possible."

Colt pushed back his hat and scratched his head. "Why not?"

She stared down into her lap. "It's a long story, but…" She squeezed her eyes tightly closed, then glanced across at him. "I was compromised. It's why my fiancée dumped me."

Colt stared at her, but only momentarily. "I'm sure it wasn't your fault. Besides, it doesn't matter to me."

Her eyes opened wide in disbelief. "Of course it does. I might as well be a soiled dove." Montana turned her face away.

Anger built up inside Colt. He was glad her back was to him so Montana couldn't see how outraged he was. Why would any man do this? It could ruin a woman for life. He tried to calm himself by silently counting to thirty. He knew ten simply wouldn't be enough. Twenty would barely make the cut either.

When he was certain his emotions were under control, Colt tapped her shoulder. "Montana," he whispered. "Look at me." She turned slowly to face him. "Do you want to talk about it?" She shook her head, and an unshed tear rolled down her cheek. Colt brushed it away, then caressed her cheek. His heart was breaking for her.

Suddenly, she began to speak, despite her earlier reluctance. "I think they set me up." That statement had his attention. "My future in-laws hated me. They wanted Lester to marry someone rich. That wasn't me. A man known for taking liberties with women cornered me in the stable." She stopped then and took a deep breath. "He tore at my clothes, and I screamed. It was then Lester pulled him away."

"Which means he knew it wasn't your fault." He stared at her curiously. "He knew that, right?"

"He did. His parents… I think they paid Rufus to attack me – to get rid of me. They told Lester he had to choose between me or his inheritance. Guess which one he chose."

Colt couldn't believe what he was hearing. How anyone could do such a thing to another person? His parents must have been really wonderful people. Dirtbags more like. "You know that doesn't matter to me, right?" He pulled Montana close and cradled her against his chest. "I love you, and that's all there is to it."

She glanced up at him then, tears flooding her cheeks. "I love you too. I don't want an annulment either."

Colt was ecstatic. He cupped her face and kissed Montana like he'd never kissed her before. *Thank you, Lord,* he said silently. *For everything.*

It didn't take long for Colt to convince his wife to return to Miss Mae's and collect her few belongings.

"I couldn't be happier," Miss Mae said, clapping her hands together. "It is way pastime someone made an honest man of our marshal." She winked at Montana then, and he enjoyed watching his wife's cheeks turn pink.

Montana hugged the elderly woman. She'd been a good friend and had lent an ear when it was needed. "I think he's already an honest man," Montana answered. "He's the finest man I've ever had the good fortune to know."

"That he is, my dear." Miss Mae looked close to tears. Surely she wasn't crying about the pair staying married? But then again, she'd been trying to marry him off for years. "You look after him, won't you?" she told Montana. "And you, Marshal, you're not making her live in that horrible marshal's cottage, are you? Besides," A sly smile came to her face then. "When the babies arrive, it will be far from big enough."

"It's time for us to go," Colt told his wife. He couldn't get her out of there fast enough.

Colt helped Montana install the last of the pretty curtains she'd made. "The cottage looks far more like a home now," he told her. The thought made him smile.

Why he'd fought against having a wife, he didn't know. But he was certain he'd made the right decision holding out. Waiting for the right person was what he really needed, and it's exactly what he got.

Montana stepped back and studied her handiwork. "I like it too. Not too feminine?" She smiled then. He'd initially told her the cottage looked *girly*. Well, it kind of did, but not in a bad way. Not once he got used to it, anyway.

It had been a matter of days since the trial was held. It had been almost six weeks since they had attacked Montana at the station, and she was finally beginning to feel like her old self. At least she told him she was, and Colt hoped that was true.

Judge Claremont was far tougher than the regular trial judge, but in this case, Colt was delighted. Montana was called to give evidence, and did it clearly and distinctly despite her distress over the entire situation. He was certain it helped with the sentencing.

Jack Tritton was to be hanged. They charged him with robbery, kidnap and murder. He'd caused the death of several women and a handful of lawmen. Colt wasn't sorry to see the end of him. The man was pure evil. They charged the rest of the gang with various offences, including robbery and kidnap. They would spend the rest of their lives in jail. If they lasted that long. Most prisoners did not take kindly to men who harmed women.

"I'm so glad that is all over," Montana said when Colt had relayed the outcome.

"I am too. They got what they deserved. Not knowing this judge didn't help. I wasn't sure which way it would go." He chuckled then. "I am pleased we weren't getting an annulment. I'm not certain he would have granted it."

"Probably not," Montana said. She turned to Colt then and hugged him. Talking about the trial was clearly stressing her out, so it was time for a change of subject.

"I've been thinking," he said. "I might clear out that spare room. You never know when it might be needed." He raised his eyebrows at her.

"You never do know," she said, a sly smile on her face.

Epilogue

Nine months later…

Montana held her husband close.

Well, as much as she could. The slow music made for a nice relaxing dance. This was the second dance Harrigan's Pass had held since she arrived. Their new preacher had made some changes, and building a closer community was one of them. Almost immediately, he'd announced a monthly dance at the church hall.

Even if she could not dance, Montana welcomed the change. She enjoyed being around people, but she particularly enjoyed spending time with her husband. Colt suddenly stopped dancing. Montana smiled as she glanced up at him. "Did you feel that?" She was chuckling now. "That was a hard kick. If I wasn't holding you, I might have toppled."

He frowned then. "I knew we should have stayed home tonight."

She shushed him. "It's fine. I'm…. Oh, no!"

Miss Mae came rushing over. She glanced about. "Colt, you go for the doc. Looks like he's not here." She stared up at him. Montana could see her husband was totally clueless. "Montana's water just broke. You're about to become a father!"

"I, er," He was dumbfounded.

"Colt!" Miss Mae near shouted then. "Pull yourself together." He had gone deathly white.

Montana was too scared to move. "Colt," she said, reaching for his hands. "I need your help. We've talked about this." He glanced down at her then and nodded.

"Right. Yes, we have. Get the doc." He picked her up and carried her to the Marshal's cottage, and gently placed her onto the bed.

Miss Mae followed along. "I'll get the water on to boil. Doc will need lots of towels as well. I'll get those ready too." She glanced about. "When is your new house going to be ready? I thought you'd be in it by now."

"It's nearly ready. I had hoped we'd be in it before the baby arrived, but it wasn't to be." Montana tried to smile between contractions, but it wasn't easy.

"You relax, my dear," Miss Mae said. Clearly, she had never birthed a baby. She returned a short time later with a pile of towels. "You've made this place look like home. I know you'll do a wonderful job of your new home. At least there you'll have far more room for the children."

"That was the idea," Montana said. "It's further out of town, as you know," she grimaced at a particularly bad contraction, "and will be lovely for our children to grow up there. Colt has resigned as marshal." Miss Mae appeared surprised. "You didn't know? I guess he hasn't announced it yet. We're taking over Mr. Hawkesbury's farm. The old man died a few weeks ago, as you know, and his son had it up for sale. We got it at a bargain price." She let out an almighty scream.

Miss Mae rolled Montana onto her side and massaged her back. It wasn't long before the doc and Colt returned.

"What's happening?" Colt asked anxiously. "I heard screaming." He looked petrified, and it worried Montana.

"What's happening is your baby is soon to make an appearance," the doc told him firmly. "Kiss your wife, then get out."

"I…"

"No husband's allowed. This is women's business," the doc told him.

Colt kissed her gently. "I love you," he said, then reluctantly left.

Some hours later, Miss Mae brought Colt home. She'd found him in the church praying. "Your daughter has arrived," Montana told him as Colt entered the bedroom.

Doc was just closing up his doctor's bag. "Congratulations," he said. "Don't linger too long. Your wife needs to rest." He handed the baby over to Colt, and he stared down into his daughter's face.

"I thought we'd call her Rose. After your mother," Montana told him wearily.

The smile on his face told Montana she'd made the right choice. *Rose Harris*. It was a beautiful name. Colt leaned in and kissed her. The expression on his face told her he was overcome with emotion.

She'd felt more contented from the moment she met Colt than she had her entire life. If she hadn't been compromised, she would never have fled. The circumstances that occurred after that were all coincidental but brutal. If they hadn't happened, she wouldn't have met Colt.

Montana was so glad the handsome marshal had saved her. She couldn't imagine her life without him. She silently prayed her thanks that everything had turned out so right for them in the end.

From the Author

Thank you so much for reading my book – I hope you enjoyed it.

I would greatly appreciate you leaving a review where you purchased, even if it is only a one-liner. It helps to have my books more visible!

About the Author

Multi-published, award-winning and bestselling author Cheryl Wright, former secretary, debt collector, account manager, writing coach, and shopping tour hostess, loves reading.

She writes both historical and contemporary western romance, as well as romantic suspense.

She lives in Melbourne, Australia, and is married with two adult children and has six grandchildren, and twin great-grandchildren.

When she's not writing, she can be found in her craft room making greeting cards.

Links

Website: *http://www.cheryl-wright.com/*

Facebook Reader Group:
https://www.facebook.com/groups/cherylwrightaut hor/

Join My Newsletter:

https://cheryl-wright.com/newsletter/
(and receive a free book)

www.ingramcontent.com/pod-product-compliance
Lightning Source LLC
Chambersburg PA
CBHW070630120726
47909CB00004B/1372